This book belongs to:

....

Note to parents and carers

Read it yourself is a series of classic, traditional tales, written in a simple way to give children a confident and successful start to reading.

Each book is carefully structured to include many high-frequency words that are vital for first reading. The sentences on each page are supported closely by pictures to help with reading, and to offer lively details to talk about.

The books are graded into four levels that progressively introduce wider vocabulary and longer stories as a reader's ability grows.

Ideas for use

- Begin by looking through the book and talking about the pictures. Has your child heard this story before?

- Help your child with any words he does not know, either by helping him to sound them out or supplying them yourself.

- Developing readers can be concentrating so hard on the words that they sometimes don't fully grasp the meaning of what they're reading. Answering the puzzle questions on pages 30 and 31 will help with understanding.

For more information and advice, visit
www.ladybird.com/readityourself

Level 1 is ideal for children who have received some initial reading instruction. Each story is told very simply, using a small number of frequently repeated words.

Special features:

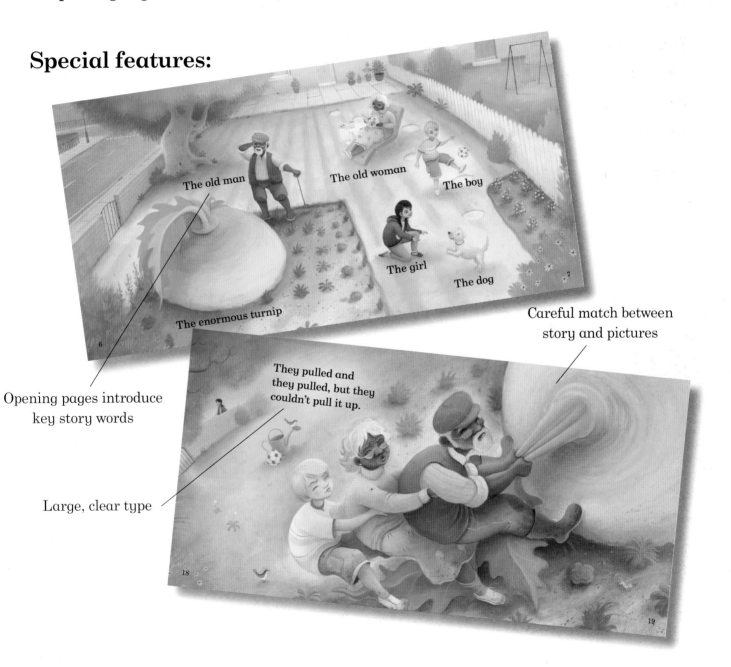

The old man

The old woman

The boy

The girl

The dog

The enormous turnip

6

7

Careful match between story and pictures

Opening pages introduce key story words

They pulled and they pulled, but they couldn't pull it up.

Large, clear type

18

19

Educational Consultant: Geraldine Taylor

A catalogue record for this book is available from the British Library

Published by Ladybird Books Ltd
80 Strand, London, WC2R 0RL
A Penguin Company

001 - 10 9 8 7 6 5 4 3 2 1
© LADYBIRD BOOKS LTD MMXI

ISBN: 978-1-40930-714-3

Printed in China

The Enormous Turnip

Illustrated by Richard Johnson

The old man

The enormous turnip

6

The old woman

The boy

The girl

The dog

7

The old man planted some turnip seeds.

The turnip seeds grew and grew.

One turnip grew enormous.

"I want that enormous turnip for my tea," said the old man.

He pulled and he pulled, but he couldn't pull it up.

The old man called
to the old woman.

"Help me pull up this
enormous turnip,"
he said.

12

13

They pulled and
they pulled, but they
couldn't pull it up.

The old woman
called to the boy.

"Help us pull up this
enormous turnip,"
she said.

They pulled and they pulled, but they couldn't pull it up.

The boy called
to the girl.

"Help us pull up this
enormous turnip,"
he said.

20

They pulled and
they pulled, but they
couldn't pull it up.

23

The girl called
to the dog.

"Help us pull up this
enormous turnip,"
she said.

They pulled and they pulled and they pulled.

Up popped the enormous turnip!

And they all had
turnip for tea.

How much do you remember about the story of The Enormous Turnip? Answer these questions and find out!

- What did the old man plant?

- Who did the old man ask to help him pull up the enormous turnip?

- Who did the girl ask to help her pull up the enormous turnip?

Look at the pictures from the story and say the order they should go in.

A

B

C

D

31

Read it yourself
with Ladybird

 The Three Billy Goats Gruff

 Cinderella

 Little Red Hen

 Goldilocks and the Three Bears

 The Enormous Turnip

 The Magic Porridge Pot

 The Ugly Duckling

 The Gingerbread Man

 Sleeping Beauty

 Little Red Riding Hood

 Sly Fox and Red Hen

 The Three Little Pigs

 Town Mouse and Country Mouse

 Chicken Licken

 The Elves and the Shoemaker

 Jack and the Beanstalk

 Hansel and Gretel

 The Pied Piper of Hamelin

 The Wizard of Oz

 Heidi

Collect all the titles in the series.